ROSEANNE
AND THE
MAGIC MIRROR

Books by the same author

Vampire Master
Spaceboy at Burlap Hall

ROSEANNE
AND THE
MAGIC MIRROR

Virginia Ironside

Illustrations by
Caroline Holden

WALKER BOOKS
LONDON

For Emily Wigglesworth

First published 1990 by Walker Books Ltd
87 Vauxhall Walk, London SE11 5HJ

Text © 1990 Virginia Ironside
Illustrations © 1990 Caroline Holden

First printed 1990
Printed and bound in Great Britain by
Richard Clay Ltd, Bungay, Suffolk

British Library Cataloguing in Publication Data
Ironside, Virginia
Roseanne and the magic mirror.
I. Title II. Holden, Caroline
823.914 [J]

ISBN 0-7445-1531-9
ISBN 0-7445-1723-0 Pbk

CONTENTS

Chapter
One

When Roseanne looked back on it, she remembered three horrible things had happened the day she got the magic mirror. Three things – if you didn't count getting up in the morning or school dinners, that is.

Getting up in the mornings was never nice when you had to go to school, and that particular day it was past half-past seven when the sun poked a long fat finger of light through the side of the curtains and on to Roseanne's pillow.

"Tick tick," went the clock, "tick tick". Then, just before the alarm went off, the clock gave a little "click" as if it was clearing its throat before it shrieked: "WAKE UP! IT'S SCHOOLTIME!"

A nasty little ache crept like a worm into Roseanne's tummy. In the bathroom the radio was playing and she could smell her dad's shaving cream. Another horrible, horrible day at school lay ahead.

It just wasn't fair. Why did everyone else

like school – except her? Why did everyone have loads of friends – except her? Why wasn't …

"Roseanne!" called her mum from downstairs. "Breakfast's ready! Time to get up!"

Breakfast. That was Horrible Thing Number One. Roseanne never wanted to eat anything on school days. She reluctantly got out of bed and stared at her school uniform. She hated that horrible blue skirt and that horrible white blouse and those horrible shoes. Why was it that school clothes looked so particularly frightful on her – and that whenever she tried to improve matters it never worked out? It was as if she didn't have any sense of style – while the other girls in her class always managed an extra touch that made them look more original.

Sharon wore a tight striped belt that matched her tie; and Gemma had got her mum to shorten her skirt so it looked quite trendy; and Annie always wore a bright scarf around her neck when they were outside the school gates so her coat didn't look so bad. But when Roseanne had tried to tie her tie into a special smart knot, she'd pulled it too tight and then she couldn't get it undone and her face had gone bright red like a party balloon and everyone had laughed at her. And when she wore some spotted socks everyone asked if she'd got measles.

When she got downstairs to the kitchen her mum was clanking around with a cup of coffee and a list. Roseanne tipped some cornflakes into a bowl and then poured some milk on to them and then she thought about eating them and then she pushed the bowl away.

Her mum stared at her crossly. "Not another tummy ache!" she said. "Your daughter's always getting tummy aches!" she said to Roseanne's dad as he came in. "And if you had a tummy ache why did you add the milk? At least you could have kept the cornflakes for tomorrow. Now they're all spoilt."

"She's a fusspot like you," said her dad. "I'll eat them."

Mum was looking at her watch and muttering: "Tsk tsk – now, shopping, ring plumber, dentist, collect car, ring council ..." Then the telephone rang and when Dad answered it he said: "What, now? Oh, good grief, I'll be in straight away," and he rushed out and Mum shouted: "Don't forget the shelving!" and then the door banged and Mum looked at her watch again and said: "Look at the time, and I'm not dressed!" while Roseanne sat at the table swinging her legs and feeling all tummy-achey and gloomy.

"Mum," she said, "I don't want to go to …"

"Roseanne! For the last time …! This happens morning after morning!" Mum was dialling a number on the phone with a pencil as she spoke. "You love school when you get there, you know you do."

"I don't," said Roseanne.

"Of course you do," said her mum. "Nonsense. Now off you go or you'll be late."

"But I don't!" said Roseanne and her eyes got all teary.

But her mum wasn't listening. "Hello? Hello?" She pulled out a drawer with one hand and wrote a list with the other hand.

"Can I stay at home?"

"It's the washing machine … the thermostat's broken …"

"Can I?"

"... if you could come in the afternoon because I'll be out in the morning ..."

"Can I?"

In the middle of Mum's conversation the bell rang. "See who that is, will you?" she said to Roseanne.

It was the milkman with his bill.

Roseanne's mum came hurrying to the door in her slippers, saying, "I'm sorry, I'm on the phone, have you got change for a tenner?"

Roseanne shifted from foot to foot and her tummy felt worse. "Can I stay at home, Mum?"

"If you haven't got the change, don't worry – put it towards next week's bill."

"Or can I come home early?"

"And an extra pint of skimmed tomorrow, Friday, please."

"Will you give me a note?"

Finally her mother stopped and, putting her hands to her head, turned to Roseanne impatiently, saying, "No, I will not and no you cannot and for heaven's sake just go to school. There's nothing wrong with you. Honestly, can't you see how busy I am …?"

Roseanne tugged on her coat slowly and miserably and pulled her satchel off the hook. She tied her shoelaces and then she shuffled down to the gate, looking back to see if Mum had changed her mind.

"Bye-bye!" called her mum, smiling now. "Have a nice day! See you later!"

She was about to shut the door when Roseanne heard her calling again. She had changed her mind! But no such luck. "I forgot," called her mother. "I won't be in when you get home so don't worry."

Roseanne tried to call back but she thought she'd cry so she didn't say anything. Her feet felt so heavy she could hardly move. Even my shoes want to stay at home, she thought.

Lessons were Horrible Thing Number Two.

"And where is your project?" asked her teacher, Miss Parker. Miss Parker wasn't really a Miss, she was a Ms, but the headmistress had told her it was too difficult for the children to say, so she had to be "Miss" in class – which made her rather cross. She never wore make-up and Roseanne didn't think she washed often because her hair was always greasy and she did pong a

bit, particularly when she leant over you to
look at your work – which this term was a
project on "Vanishing Species in the Animal
World".

"You said you didn't want it in till
Thursday," said Roseanne.

"And what day do you think it is today,
Roseanne?" Everyone laughed and Miss
Parker smiled a chilly smile. "Sunday?"
Everyone laughed again.

"Thursday," said Roseanne, suddenly
realizing and going pink. "I left it at home.

But I've done another two pages, I really have."

"Yes, I'm sure you have," said Miss Parker, curling her lip and meaning she was sure she hadn't. "Has your memory gone on holiday by any chance? Is it lying in the sun on a faraway beach when it should be at school?"

The whole class laughed again. Roseanne thought that the sound of everyone laughing at a teacher's unkind joke was the most horrible sound in the world.

"Please bring it in tomorrow," said Miss Parker, "and make a special point of showing it to me. This has happened before and it mustn't happen again."

"No, Miss Parker." Roseanne felt very small.

"And remember to bring your memory to school as well tomorrow, please!"

Everyone laughed and laughed.

School dinner was always nasty but today it was sausages and Roseanne hated sausages because the school ones had horrible gristly bits in the middle that you couldn't see until you got them in your mouth and they surprised you by making your teeth jump. They were accompanied by slimy beans.

"Beans can't be slimy!" her mum had said. But the school cooks managed to make them slimy. They probably had a special slimy beans recipe. Roseanne sometimes imagined the school cooks talking to each other at school cooks' meetings:

"Could I have your recipe for special gristly sausages?"

"Certainly, if you would kindly give me the recipe for lumpy gravy. My gravy always comes out too smooth."

"Of course. And I've just discovered how to make really soggy pale chips, too – such a change from the crisp golden ones."

"Mm, delicious! Just right to have with gluey spaghetti! And if you tell me how you get the skin on your custard, I'll tell you the secret of how to make Yorkshire puddings like flat, old shoe-leather."

* * *

Sharon's party invitations were Horrible Thing Number Three. When she handed them out in the playground at the end of the day, Roseanne sat down on a bench and tried not to watch. She just hoped and hoped she'd be invited but she hardly ever got asked to people's parties. It wasn't so much that she was unpopular, it was more that people seemed to forget about her and made excuses.

"Didn't you get my invitation? Oh, I thought I gave you one!" "I seem to have left your invitation at home – sorry. I'll give you the address and the time in a minute" – but something always made them forget. "You were ill when I gave the invitations out and yours must have got lost – I'm really sorry. We had a terrific time, too" – and so on.

"There's one for you, Annie," Sharon was saying. "Yes, we've got a special children's entertainer called Uncle Jim. He makes balloons into animals and he gets a rabbit out of a hat."

"A real rabbit?"

"Yes, a real rabbit! Gemma, here's yours –
we're all dressing up as pop stars."

"Oooh!"

Roseanne wished and wished she'd get an
invitation. She stared at the ground and the
white lines painted on it for netball and she
felt tears come to her eyes. Then she heard a
whispering behind her and the sound of steps.
She looked up very slowly. It was Sharon.

Was she going to get an invitation after all?

"Roseanne, I'm sorry," said Sharon, "but my mum says I can only have twenty people to my party because we haven't got enough room and I had to leave someone out so I'm afraid … but if someone can't come, then I'll ask you, I promise."

Roseanne tried to smile but she felt too disappointed and hurt. Her tummy started to

ache again and she rushed out of the playground and into the loo where she just sat and cried and cried.

Why couldn't Sharon's mum just squeeze in one more person? She wasn't very big. She could lose weight before the party and she'd be even smaller. She wouldn't eat very much. In fact she wouldn't eat anything at all. She just wanted to see the conjuror make the balloons into animals and see him bring a rabbit out of a hat. What was wrong with her? Why didn't anyone seem to notice her or care about her?

"I wish," she said to herself, "I wish I could go to the party. If only I could be really clever and nice maybe people would notice me – or maybe if I could be really funny and daring, that would work. I just wish I knew what was wrong with me."

At the sound of footsteps outside, she pulled the chain in the loo to pretend she'd been, and picked up her satchel.

But something funny had happened. Her

satchel was much, much heavier than it had been before. It was as if it contained a big stone. She undid the buckle and looked inside.

There was a huge, flat parcel wrapped up in brown paper. Odder still, it had the name "Roseanne" written on it.

What on earth could it be? And how had it got there? She certainly hadn't put it there – and before she'd gone to the loo her satchel had been just the same weight as usual, of that she was as certain as could be. She looked around. Could someone have pulled her satchel under the partition and stuffed the parcel in and then pushed it back? No – the gap was too small.

"Time to go home!" Miss Parker banged on the door. "We're locking up. You don't want to stay in school all night!"

"Sorry," said Roseanne, coming out and brushing her hand across her eyes to wipe away the tears. She pushed past the teacher and set off home. But she felt different. Even though her satchel was so much heavier, there was a spring in her step.

She just couldn't wait to open the mysterious package.

Chapter
Two

The note from Roseanne's mum on the kitchen table read:

I'u be back
at six.
There's cake
and milk
in the fridge.

But Roseanne was far too excited about her parcel to bother with the cake and she raced upstairs to her room without even bothering to take off her coat. She opened her satchel with trembling hands and slowly pulled out the package. It was very, very heavy and tied up with string which was odd, because you don't see a lot of parcels tied up with string these days. She undid the knots and pulled away the paper.

What could it be? A make-up set? A junior post-office? (She hoped it wasn't a junior post-office because she'd already got one and it was really boring.) Or could it be a ping-pong-table set – or some books?

It wasn't any of those things. It wasn't even

like any of those things.

It was a big mirror, with two rectangular mirrors hinged to each side. And as she looked at it, Roseanne saw her astonished face reflected in the glass.

"What on earth is this?" she said to herself. "Why should anyone give me a mirror? And why are there three bits?"

She'd only once seen a mirror like it before, in an old black-and-white TV film. An old-fashioned movie star had been sitting in front of it combing her hair and sipping a drink. Roseanne remembered that the mirror stood up on the dressing table so the star could see herself from all sides.

With difficulty, Roseanne lifted the heavy mirror and put it on the table under her window. The wooden frame was carved with owls and cats and leaves and moons, which had been brushed with gold paint. Inlaid were mother-of-pearl stars and strange symbols.

It must be very, very old – a real antique, thought Roseanne as she leaned over to examine it.

She pulled the two sides towards her and looked. She could see the front of her face in the centre bit and she could see the left side of her face in the left-hand bit and the right side in the right-hand bit. But the images weren't very clear; it was as if dirt had got in behind the glass and made the reflections a fuzzy, greyish-blue.

But as the evening started to draw in and Roseanne went to turn on her lamp, she noticed a strange, hazy, silvery light glowing from the three mirrors. The tummy ache she'd had that morning had completely disappeared and was replaced by an excited, jumpy feeling inside.

"Roseanne! Roseanne!" Her thoughts were interrupted by her mother's voice from downstairs. "I'm back!" Then there was a jostling sound of shopping being unloaded in the kitchen and cupboard doors being opened and then a surprised: "But darling, you haven't eaten your tea! And you've still got your coat on!" she added, when she saw Roseanne coming down the stairs. "But it's not cold and you must have been back ages ago! Are you ill?" Mum put her hand on Roseanne's forehead. "There's nothing wrong with you at all!" she snapped rather crossly. "If you think you can get out of going to school tomorrow by pretending to be ill, you're mistaken!"

Roseanne took off her coat and hung it up and got her cake from the fridge. "No, I'm fine," she said. "But something very funny happened to me. I got this strange pres ..."

But at that moment the telephone rang and then the cat started miaowing for his supper and Mum sighed and put her hand to her head and said, "Feed him, will you? Now who can this be? I've got to go out tonight to meet Dad, but we won't be late and Mrs Exmoor's next door if you need her and ... Hello! Oh, how are you! Long time no see! I've just got in but let me just get my cup of coffee and find my diary ..."

She grabbed her coffee and went to the phone in the next room leaving Roseanne alone to eat her cake, her legs dangling from her chair. Oh, well. No one was very interested in what happened to her. And anyway, maybe she'd better keep quiet about the mirror. Mum might want it for herself, or she might say she should take it to the police because it could be stolen property or she might just say: "Oh yes, very nice!" in a vague way as if she were thinking about something else and that would make Roseanne feel all sad and flat. No, she'd keep her mysterious present a secret.

Roseanne didn't like it when her mum and dad went out. They couldn't afford a babysitter, so she was left to fend for herself. Someone at school had said it was against the law to leave children on their own for long periods but she'd never liked to say anything because she knew her mother was so busy.

And her parents had kept the old baby

alarm they'd used when she was tiny and
they'd strung it between their house and next
door, so if Mrs Exmoor heard Roseanne call
she'd come over straight away. But it wasn't
the same as someone else being in the house –
though Roseanne didn't mind too much
because she'd never seen a ghost or a burglar.

But this particular night, when she'd had
her milk and got into bed and fallen asleep,
she had a real shock. She was just in the

middle of a lovely dream (in which she had turned into one of the dinner ladies and all the real dinner ladies were sitting at the table being forced to eat disgusting school food) when she was woken by sounds in her room.

Roseanne peeped over the top of her duvet and listened. Nothing. Then, just as she was nodding off again and planning to give the dinner ladies a real surprise by serving them up some apple pie which was all thick soggy pastry and just a thin scraping of apple sauce in the middle, she heard voices.

"Roseanne! Roseanne," whispered one voice. It was very sweet and piping. "Dear Roseanne, wake from your sleep!"

Roseanne woke up again with a start. Was Mum back early? No, because in the darkness she could see that the light wasn't on in the hall, which always meant that her parents had returned.

She stared into the darkness and clutched her duvet in panic.

"Roseanne! My dear! Wake up!" Then this voice was interrupted by another voice –

a different voice, extremely cross and bad-tempered. "Oh, for heaven's sake, Roseanne, stop fooling around. Just wake up!"

Roseanne froze. Slowly she turned round, peering desperately into the blackness of her room. She couldn't make anything out in the darkness except the vague shape of her chair and the folds of her curtains. There was no noise except her heart thumping like a military drum. She was sure there was no one there – and then she saw a funny silvery light in the corner.

"Yes, yes, over here!" said the two voices. The silvery light got brighter and suddenly she saw that it was coming from her new mirror. She held her breath. At least it wasn't burglars. She slid out of bed, tiptoed over to her table and stared into the glass.

And there, to her utter amazement, she saw three clear reflections. In the centre she saw herself in her nightdress, looking extremely mystified and anxious. But in the left-hand mirror there was someone else.

Or was it?

It looked like her but a different sort of her.
It was a rather cross and cheeky-looking girl
with dirty, tousled hair and a big frown – and
yet her eyes were twinkling all the same. And
in the right-hand mirror was someone else
again, another girl who looked like her – but
this one had a saintly expression on her face
and hair which was brushed till it gleamed.
And it was she who spoke first.

"Good evening, Roseanne. Let me introduce myself." She smiled, smugly. "I'm Anne." She stretched out her hand as if to shake Roseanne's but when Roseanne offered hers in return it just bumped against the glass.

"And I'm Rose," shouted the other one from the left-hand mirror. She gave a cunning grin.

"We're Roseanne," they said together.

"No, I'm Roseanne!" cried Roseanne.

"You're rather one-dimensional, if you'll excuse me saying so," said Anne. "We are your other dimensions, which make you more – more like a whole human being."

"In other words," Rose butted in rudely, "you're the boring bit!"

Anne shot Rose a disapproving look. "It's not kind to say that sort of thing," she said. "No," she added, turning back to Roseanne, "you're the Roseanne who hasn't reached her full potential yet. You are like a young bud, that has not yet turned into a beautiful flower."

"Do you, mind," said Rose, making a face. "I can't bear listening to this cr …"

"Rose!" said Anne, reprovingly. "Manners!" Again she turned to Roseanne. "I am the petals of the flower, the sweet perfume at eventide, the lustrous colour and the drop of dew. Rose, on the other hand, is the thorn on your stem and the dirty root in the ground."

"Thanks a million!" snapped Rose at Anne. Then she turned to Roseanne. "You know the reason no one really notices you at school? It's because you've got no personality. No fun and games. No – well, let's put it this way. You're not exactly full of beans. I'm the beans you should be full of."

Anne shook her head despairingly. "I doubt, Rose, if Roseanne wishes to be full of beans. They would only make her burp. No, Roseanne, you should be full of goodness. And I'm here to show you the good bits of you," said Anne quietly. "I am here to help you be kind and thoughtful and clean and hardworking, so everyone will love you."

"And I," said Rose, jabbing a finger rudely at Roseanne, "I'm here because I want you to have loads of fun and get up to all kinds of tricks and have millions of friends."

In the reflection, Rose picked up the corner of her nightdress and blew her nose on it. Anne, on the other side, winced at the sight. Rose noticed this and stuck out her tongue at her.

"I hate Anne because she's a stuck-up, perfect little prig," said Rose, sneering.

"And I don't hate anyone because I'm so good," said Anne. "But I cannot say I approve of Rose – she is so bad-mannered and naughty." And she patted a stray lock of hair into place.

"What are you doing here?" asked Roseanne, staring at each of them.

"Well, you said you wanted to know what was wrong with you," said Rose. "You said – and I quote – 'If only I could be really clever and nice maybe people would notice me – or maybe if I could be really funny and daring, that would work.' So here we are. Now's your chance." She picked her nose and then stuck a finger in an ear and looked at it to see if there was any wax on it.

"Yes, I'm your good side," said Anne.

"And I'm your bad side," said Rose.

"And we have come to fulfil your wish," said Anne, carefully smoothing out a tiny wrinkle she had noticed on her nightdress.

"All you have to do is to choose one of us for a week to see which you prefer."

"What do you mean, choose one of you for a week?" said Roseanne, frowning. She wasn't certain she wanted to choose either of them.

"Choose one of us!" barked Rose. "Can't you hear, cloth-ears? You deaf or something? What do you call two raincoats in a cemetery?"

"It's only for a week," said Anne, gently ignoring Rose's question. "Then you can always choose the other one."

"What *do* you call two raincoats in a cemetery?" asked Roseanne, curious.

"Max Bygraves!" yelled Rose. "Choose me first!"

"Obviously I would prefer it if you were to choose me first, but I must leave the decision up to you," said Anne, politely.

"But," they both said together, "you must choose one of us. So which is it to be?"

Chapter
Three

Roseanne looked from one to the other. Rose was now making faces and putting her thumbs in her ears and wiggling her fingers; Anne was sitting calm and poised and humming a quiet hymn to herself.

Rose had an attractive little gleam in her eye and she certainly looked a lot more fun than Anne; but if Roseanne became Rose for a week she might get into trouble at school! Maybe if she became Anne, people would like her because she'd be good and kind.

"I think I'll choose – Anne," she said.

She wasn't expecting Rose's reaction. Rose screamed and yelled and tore her hair and banged on the glass. "I hate you, I hate you!" she screamed. "You're the stupidest doopidest person I've ever met!" Then she burst into furious tears and kept sniffing.

Anne, in the meanwhile, turned to Roseanne with a saintly smile. "You've made the right choice, my dear," she said gently. "Now just go back to sleep and tomorrow morning you'll wake up and you'll be me."

Roseanne crept back into bed wondering if she'd been dreaming. The angry sobs from Rose grew fainter and fainter and slowly Roseanne drifted into a deep sleep.

The next morning she woke before the alarm had a chance to go off. She found herself bouncing out of bed humming, "If you want to make it happy clap your hands". She brushed and brushed her hair till it gleamed; she picked up her project and put it into her satchel which she carefully dusted before skipping downstairs.

In the kitchen Roseanne found herself drawing the curtains and putting on the kettle and starting to make the breakfast for her mum and dad. She'd never done it before but to her astonishment she could do everything perfectly and she even put out a clean sheet of kitchen towel by everyone's place so they could wipe their mouths if they got butter on their lips. As she heard her mother come stumping down the stairs she called out, "Good morning, Mama!" and her mum came in looking extremely cross and suspicious.

"Mama! You've never called me that before!" she said, irritably. "Now sit down, I've got breakfast to make."

"A little fairy has been here before you," Roseanne heard herself saying, coyly. It was rather unnerving hearing this sort of thing coming out of her mouth. "It's a special treat for you, Mother, dear. Now sit down and relax while I pour the tea."

"WHAT!" said Mum, completely astonished. But she sat down anyway and looked at Roseanne in amazement. "What is all this? And why are you up so early? If you think you can wriggle out of school by making breakfast you're mistaken!"

"Wriggle out of school?" Roseanne heard herself say in a shocked voice as she sat down. "Me? I'm up particularly early because I want to get there on time. In fact I'd like to be early so I can polish my desk."

Roseanne could hardly believe she was hearing right. But she helped herself to cornflakes, added milk, and ate up every scrap. Mum was still gazing at her, struck dumb with astonishment, when Dad came down.

"You finished already?" he said, rather crossly.

"Yes, Roseanne's made the breakfast for us," said Mum, making a face at him as if she was trying to tell him something privately.

"Made the breakfast!" said Dad. "Well,

that's nice, I must say." He glanced up at
Roseanne. "Good heavens you are looking
nice, pet. Just look at your shining hair – and
you're dressed neatly for once."

Roseanne smiled smugly. She felt quite
pleased about all this. It wasn't so bad being
Anne after all. But then she heard herself
speaking.

"Now, I have something to say to you both
that you may not like, but I feel I have to say
it," she said. "I'm not sure if you are aware of
this but it isn't right to leave me on my own
at night when you go out – with only the

baby alarm to Mrs Exmoor's. It's not against the law, but were anything to happen to me, you might be had up by the police for negligence. You shouldn't do it in future. And I think you ought to get earlier nights, as well. You both look very tired to me and I don't want my parents getting ill."

Both Mum and Dad gawped at this speech.

"Oh, listen to Miss Goody-two-shoes!" said Mum. "And who'll pay for this babysitter, pray?"

"Dad could always work an extra hour overtime," Roseanne heard Anne saying out of her mouth. Her father choked on his coffee. "Or you could go out less often. And I'm willing to make a contribution from my pocket-money." Half-way through this last sentence Roseanne tried to clap a hand over her mouth as she realized what she was about to say but her hands felt terribly heavy and she couldn't get them up to her face in time. She tried to say she didn't mean it but however much she moved her lips no sound would come out. For the first time Roseanne felt rather frightened. Anne was in complete control; goodness knows what dreadful things she might say or do next.

Mum got up and felt Roseanne's forehead. "You know, Dad, I think your daughter really is ill this time. Are you sure you feel well enough to go to school?"

Roseanne couldn't believe her clean ears. But her hopes of getting off school were dashed by Anne saying: "Of course I'm well enough. There is nothing wrong with me."

"Mrs Exmoor said she heard talking from her bedroom last night," said Mum to Dad worriedly. "Do you think someone crept in and got to Roseanne? Some religious maniac?"

Roseanne heard a laugh tinkling from her lips. "No, that was just me and my friends," she said. "Having a little chat after lights out!"

"She *is* ill," said Mum. "I'm taking you to the doctor's straight away – no arguments!"

* * *

"There's nothing wrong with her at all," said the doctor, crossly, after he'd examined Roseanne. "She is a charming, well-adjusted child and you ought to be proud of her."

Mum thanked him and was about to leave when Roseanne felt herself clearing her throat. She dreaded what Anne might say, and well she might because – "Excuse me," she heard herself say. "I'd just like you to have a word with my mum about her smoking. I feel it is very dangerous …"

But Mum had pulled Roseanne away, saying she had to get to school.

Outside she turned on her daughter. "How dare you go on about my smoking!"

"I have to say what I feel is right," said Roseanne piously.

Much to Roseanne's embarrassment the prissy behaviour continued even at school.

"I quite understand why there is no room for me at your party, Sharon," she told her classmate in the playground. Quite understand? What on earth was she saying? She didn't understand at all – in fact she still felt pretty angry and upset at being left out. "I hope it's a great success, however, and even though I'm not coming I'd like to buy you a nice present. And will you tell your mother that if she wants any help with the sandwiches I would be delighted to lend a hand. Of course I won't expect to attend as I know there isn't room for me."

Sharon stared at her, obviously thinking

this suggestion was quite mad. "Er – thanks," she said, doubtfully. "Brought your project in today?"

"I certainly have," replied Roseanne, neatly pulling up her socks which had fallen down.

"Me and Wendy are copying most of ours from the children's encyclopaedia," giggled Sharon. She seemed quite friendly – probably, Roseanne thought, because she knew she was getting an extra present.

Inside herself, Roseanne felt Anne's disapproval about the copying out, but she managed to say nothing except a vague: "Oh, really?" She didn't think Sharon would like being told that it wasn't right to cheat.

She hoped Anne had forgotten about it, too. And indeed she seemed to have, until Miss Parker asked to see her project.

"But this is very good work!" she exclaimed when she saw it. "Now this is more like it Roseanne." Even though the extra pages were work she had done before she'd been taken over by Anne, Roseanne wondered if she'd have got as much praise from Miss Parker if she'd still been her ordinary old self. She could see Miss Parker liked her new neat look and her quiet attention to everything being said in class. "Well done! You'll really enjoy next week's trip to the museum where we'll be studying animals and the vanishing species in much greater depth."

"Thank you," said Anne through Roseanne, smiling prettily at the compliments. "I thought it was best to do original work. I'm afraid Sharon and Wendy have been cheating, Miss Parker, and" – at this point Roseanne felt a silent groan of horror rise up in herself as she realized what Anne was about to say – "and copying bits out of a children's encyclopaedia."

There was a horrified gasp from the class.

"Cheating, eh?" said Miss Parker, staring coldly at Sharon and Wendy. "Let me have another look at those projects, you two …"

* * *

At dinner-time Anne made Roseanne eat up
every scrap of meatloaf even though it tasted
as if it had been made from yucky bits
scraped off the pavement. Instead of leaving
the lumps in her gravy, she ate them too. It
really was disgusting and she wished Anne
wasn't so good because in the end she felt her
tummy heaving. To make matters even worse
she found herself getting up from the table
with her plate and actually begging the dinner
ladies for a second helping, something she'd
never done in her life before.

"I'm afraid I can't resist having another
delicious portion," she heard Anne say, while
inside herself wondering how on earth she'd
keep the stuff down.

By the time she'd choked back the second helping her tummy was really aching – but that was probably partly due to the fact that she had a feeling she wouldn't get away with telling tales about Sharon and Wendy's project.

And how right she was. They were waiting for her in the playground after school looking extremely angry and threatening.

"Tell-tale tit, your tongue shall be slit," said Sharon, pulling her hair.

"We'll teach you to tell tales," said Wendy, yanking Roseanne's satchel off her back.

Then they both jumped on Roseanne and scratched her and screamed at her until her hair was all messy and muddy and her clothes torn and streaked with dirt. Worst of all, they took her project and ripped it into tiny pieces and dashed off to flush it down the loo.

Her torn clothes streaked with mud, Roseanne sat panting on the school bench. Inside herself she felt like crying, but Anne preserved a calm, poised front to the world.

How would she survive the next few days? Being Anne certainly didn't make her more popular. It had been an absolutely disastrous choice. OK, the teachers seemed keener on her than before, but she'd be lucky if her classmates ever spoke to her again – and she could hardly blame them.

And at this rate, anyway, with the wrecked school uniform, the teachers would soon turn against her as well. And what would her mum say?

Forlornly, she picked up her things and brushed herself down. Although Anne tried to make her visit the headmistress to tell further tales of Sharon and Wendy's latest behaviour, the plan came unstuck because the head, thank goodness, was in a meeting and couldn't be disturbed.

Much to Roseanne's relief, Anne decided to return home, but she was still anxious about how she could explain the state of her clothes to her mum.

But Mum wasn't in and Roseanne found

herself rushing round the kitchen sorting out the washing powder and the washing machine instructions and reading how it worked. First she stripped off all her clothes and put them in the machine, then tumbled upstairs into a bath and shampooed her hair. She neatly mended the tears in her clothes when they were dry with a dexterity with the needle and thread she never imagined she possessed and by the time her mum came back no one would have known she had been in a fight. Not only was she as neat and spotless as she had been that morning – indeed even more so if that was possible – but she'd somehow managed to find the time to rustle up some delicious currant scones for tea. Anne was certainly a good cook and even Roseanne could hardly wait to sit down and gobble them up.

"Nice day at school?" asked her mum when she had got in and congratulated Roseanne on her scone-making.

"Lovely," replied the Anne inside

Roseanne. "I'm only sorry that tomorrow is the weekend. However, I've got plenty of work to do. And Mother – I'm rather concerned." Concerned? Roseanne shook inside. What ghastly idea did Anne have in mind now? She soon knew. "Why have I never been taken to Sunday School? I'd be ever so grateful, if it's not too much trouble, if you could arrange that."

Work! Sunday School! Roseanne was powerless to prevent Anne's plans. The work Anne had in mind was to re-write her project entirely from beginning to end. Roseanne worked late into the night, so late that she was still hard at it when the mirror woke up. Rose started screaming again.

"You should have chosen me! Look where Anne's got you! You stupid nerd! Let me out! Let me out!"

Even though privately Roseanne agreed with every word Rose said, eventually she was forced to put a blanket over the mirror to muffle Rose's voice.

On Sunday she went to Sunday School, came back and helped wash up the lunch dishes and then went back to work on her project. On Monday she was so unpopular at school that no one would speak to her so at least she was left in comparative peace. She helped blind people and old ladies across roads and swept the front path and tidied her room and behaved extremely well when relations came to tea. But she did wish that Anne hadn't made her curtsy as they left, because her whole family had burst out laughing.

When she leant out of her upstairs window to wave goodbye to them, she overheard her uncle and aunt discussing her down the path. "A delightful girl," he said, "but rather unnaturally good don't you think?"

"Weird," her aunt had said. "I like a child with a bit more life in her. But, I did appreciate the little pen-wiper she made for me."

And when the week was up, Roseanne was

incredibly relieved. She was so fed up with being good that she could have popped.

The voices came again in the middle of the night, calling to her. The Anne in her had vanished back into the mirror and Roseanne was at last her old self. She hopped out of bed to the mirror and there were Rose and Anne, both peering out.

"I hope you enjoyed being me," said Anne, smiling. "You can always choose me again for another week, you know. You don't have to choose Rose."

Roseanne's heart sank. "Well, thank you, but although I enjoyed bits of being you, like making the scones and helping blind people and I even quite enjoyed re-doing my project, I didn't like telling tales or Sunday School or making the breakfast every morning and doing quite so much house-work. And I didn't enjoy eating up my lunch every day."

"No chance of that with me!" yelled Rose roaring with laughter from the mirror. "I

wouldn't eat that yuk if you paid me! And
I've got some some really good jokes, too. But
of course there's a chance we won't be at
school much because it'd be nice to play
truant, eh?"

When Roseanne looked at her slightly
nervously, she changed her story. "No, don't
worry. I was only kidding," she said, giggling.

"I'm afraid, dear Roseanne, you can't
believe a word Rose says. I don't like to say

it, but she is a compulsive liar," said Anne, sighing.

"I must give her a turn, though," said Roseanne, thinking she'd rather be anything than Anne again. And Rose was a good laugh in her way. "Otherwise she'll be screaming the place down every night," she added, tactfully.

"Have it your own way, my dear," said Anne. "But don't say I didn't warn you."

Chapter
Four

The next morning Roseanne tried to get out
of bed on time but Rose just wouldn't let her.
Every time she attempted to force her feet out
onto the floor, she could hear Rose inside her
saying: "Naw – stay in bed and have a bit more
of a kip. You're too tired to go to school."

Eventually her mum came upstairs and
actually pulled off her bedclothes before
Roseanne heard herself say: "Go away!
Haven't you got anything better to do? I'm
tired! Leave me alone!"

"If you talk to me like that you won't get
any breakfast," said her mother. "And anyway,
what's happened to you? Last week you
were so good – and now you refuse to get out
of bed!"

Rose stuck out her tongue at Roseanne's
mother and sang out: "Ner, ner, ner-ner, ner!
I don't want any breakfast, so ner!"

"And what," said Roseanne's mother, tight-
lipped as she gathered Roseanne's school
clothes together, "does 'ner, ner, ner-ner, ner'
mean?"

"It means 'ner, ner, ner-ner, ner' you nerd, so ner!" Roseanne heard herself saying. "Glad I'm not having breakfast. Your breakfast's yuk!"

Roseanne's mother was so astonished at hearing this that she said nothing, but left her to it. When Roseanne came down to the kitchen she heard her father saying " ... probably just a phase" through the door.

Roseanne burst through the door, her hair uncombed and her laces untied. "It is not a phase," she yelled. "I'm going to be like this for ever and ever, so stuff that up your jumper with knobs on!"

Roseanne was shocked to hear the way she spoke to her dad. She was also horrified at the confident way Rose assumed she would never choose to be anyone but Rose for the rest of her life. Luckily, she noticed her dad trying hard to resist a smile. Eventually he started to laugh. "Roseanne, I've never seen you like this before," he said. "What on earth's got into you?"

Roseanne wished she could tell him that Rose had got into her, but she couldn't answer and just silently banged her way into the hall and went out, trailing her coat along the path in the puddles.

"Put your coat on at once!" called her mother angrily from the door. "I'm not going to pay for it to be cleaned!"

*   *   *

Although no one was speaking to Roseanne at school because she'd been such a tell-tale the week before, it didn't take long before Rose had won them over. It started when she said to Miss Parker, who was writing something on the blackboard: "Oh, Miss, tickle your bottom with a feather!"

The whole class shook with suppressed giggles but when Miss Parker whirled round and said, "What did you say?" Rose replied, "Oh, particularly rotten weather, Miss, for the time of year, don't you think?"

All Roseanne's past priggishness was forgotten and when they set off on their expedition to the natural history museum to make notes for their projects, no less than three people wanted to be Roseanne's partner.

"How do you get two whales in a car?" she asked Annie, who was lucky enough to be paired up with her.

"Dunno."

"On the M4!"

"Don't get it," said Annie, after a while.

"Two whales – to Wales – in a car!" explained Rose, impatiently.

"Now you must be extremely sensible," Miss Parker had warned the class before they set out. "I want you all to behave impeccably – no running or noisiness in the museum. Understand?"

"I understand!" yelled Rose so loudly that the whole class had to put their hands over their ears. Miss Parker pointed at her severely. Roseanne immediately turned round and looked behind her, looking for what Miss

Parker seemed to be pointing at.

"Roseanne! You! Be quiet! Do you hear?"

"Yes," whispered Rose so quietly only her neighbours could hear her.

"I said, did you hear?" snapped Miss Parker.

"Yes," whispered Rose again, so quietly that even she couldn't hear herself.

"DID YOU HEAR ME?" roared Miss Parker furiously.

Rose put her finger to her lips. "I thought you said to be quiet, Miss," she whispered.

"What?" said Miss Parker.

"I THOUGHT YOU SAID TO BE QUIET MISS!" screamed Rose, making Miss Parker jump. The teacher pursed her lips.

At the museum there were stuffed monkeys, stuffed elephants, stuffed llamas (going a bit bald on top) and stuffed rabbits and mice. There were birds' eggs and dried insects and rows of larvae and pupae and different nests in glass cases. There was even a dinosaur reconstructed out of old bones.

After a while, when, for the third time, Miss Parker had explained to everyone how a hedgehog rolls itself up into a ball to protect itself, Roseanne got bored with looking and slipped away to the room where the stuffed monkeys were.

She stood in front of the orang-utan – and then she noticed that the doors to its glass case had hinges on it. She could get inside! The last thing Roseanne wanted to do was to get inside a glass case with a stuffed orang-utan, but Rose insisted she pull open one of the glass doors and slip in. Running down the orang-utan's back, hidden by plastic leaves, was a big long zip – and Rose mischievously undid it and started pulling out just enough stuffing for Roseanne to wriggle inside. She tried her best to resist but her arms and legs had a mind of their own – or rather a mind of Rose's – and there was nothing she could do to stop them.

It was hot and prickly inside the orang-utan and Roseanne felt miserable, listening to Miss

Parker calling for her again and again. Maybe she'd be trapped in the museum overnight! Maybe she'd never get out! Maybe she'd die in there! Finally the teacher came into the monkey room and looked about with the rest of the class.

"Roseanne! Where are you! We're going back now!"

With horror Roseanne realized that Rose wasn't going to move until the class had actually turned and were leaving the room. But, almost worse than being left on her own, was when Rose decided to let out a slow, throaty grunt. Miss Parker whirled round suspiciously. Roseanne followed up the grunt

with another louder grunt and slowly started scratching under her arm.

"Help!" cried Wendy, "It's alive!" She raced out of the room, knocking over a cabinet of priceless birds' nests which all fell on the floor, a mass of twigs and broken glass.

Inside the glass case, Roseanne found herself jumping up and down in her hairy orang-utan's suit, while the class watched, transfixed. Miss Parker stood frozen with fear. And when Rose pushed open the hinged door and lunged out going: "URGH URGH URGH", the teacher passed out completely and the whole class started screaming.

Museum keepers came running from all directions and were appalled when they found out who had unpicked their orang-utan. And although Sharon and Gemma looked at Roseanne with a strange sort of respect, as she stepped out of the suit covered with bits of cotton wool and straw, she heard Sharon whispering, "I'm glad she's not coming to my party. Mum would have a fit if anything like that happened!"

"Well I'm glad I'm not coming to your party if your living room's filled with stuffed monkeys!" said Rose rudely.

The moment the class returned to school Roseanne's parents were summoned and Roseanne was sent home in disgrace.

"I wish I'd seen you," said Dad, when he got home. Although he'd tried to play the heavy-handed father, he couldn't help finding it all rather funny.

"It's not amusing," said her mum, angrily. "The museum people say they're going to

send us the bill for restuffing their orang-utan
– and Wendy's parents have just been on to us
absolutely furious because the museum has
sent them a bill for that cabinet of birds' nests
and it'll cost a lot to replace, they say."

At the mention of money, Roseanne's dad
looked very stern. "So what are you going to
do about it?" he said to Roseanne. "The least
you could do is write a letter of apology."

So Roseanne was made to write a very neat
letter saying how sorry she was to the
museum people.

Could the week have got any worse?

Hardly. Roseanne found herself throwing buns down the dining-table, cheating at her work, putting worms in Miss Parker's lunch, and fighting everyone in the playground. When she found herself in a sweet-shop and the shop-keeper wasn't looking, to her utter horror, she took a chocolate bar from the shelf and popped it in her pocket. This was perhaps the worst moment of all of being Rose. Roseanne was convinced the shop-keeper would spot her and call the police but luckily he didn't seem to notice. Although on the outside Rose was laughing and joking, inside herself Roseanne mentally held her head in her hands with her eyes tight shut, unable to bear any more of Rose's capers.

Every night she could hear Anne sighing from the mirror: "I told you so!" and "That's what comes of not taking my advice!" and "I said you'd be sorry" and every night Roseanne tossed and turned, just dreading another day of being Rose. She had nightmares about being sent to a special

school for problem children and every time the bell rang she was scared stiff that there would be a policeman waiting with a pair of handcuffs to take her to the cells, charging her with stealing a chocolate bar from the shop.

Once she heard her parents downstairs, discussing her. Her mother was getting more and more worried.

"Don't look at me, she's your daughter," she heard her dad say.

"My daughter!" she heard her mum reply furiously. "She's your daughter! She takes after your side of the family. Remember your Aunt Jezebel!"

"Your Cousin Viler was no better!"

"She wasn't called Viler, she was called Viola!" snapped her mother.

Roseanne just couldn't wait for the end of the week. Although she had hated being Anne, at least she didn't upset her mum and dad so much. But really, she'd just much rather be Roseanne.

The last day finally came and Roseanne sank thankfully into bed. She tried to sleep but she was too anxious. If by any chance she slept through that night she worried that she might be stuck with being Rose for another week and if she had to be Rose one minute longer she didn't know what she would do.

But eventually, at around midnight, the voices started again.

"Roseanne, Roseanne, what will be your choice for this week?"

"Come on, you sluggabed!" yelled Rose. "We had good fun this week, didn't we? Let's go on for another week."

Roseanne slipped out of bed and tiptoed over to the mirror in her nightdress. She sat in front of it, looking from one reflection to the other, from Rose to Anne, each staring out from the silvery glow.

She definitely didn't want to be Rose. But there again – Anne. Could she really stand being that prissy little tell-tale for another week?

If only she'd never got the magic mirror. A tear stole down her cheek. She knew she had to choose. But which was it to be?

Chapter
Five

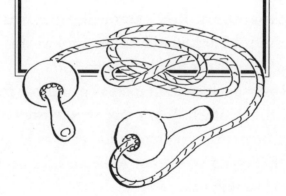

"Cry-baby cry!" taunted Rose, sneering at her from her side of the mirror. "Snivelling won't get you anywhere. Pull yourself together and stop being such a wimp!"

"Oh, my poor, poor, dear," murmured Anne, her face bursting with sympathy. "But the answer's quite simple. Just choose me."

"Her!" screamed Rose, pointing at Anne across her glass. "Her! That horrible goody-goody! Ugh! I'd like to scratch her eyes out!"

At this Anne simply turned her back and said: "I don't wish to listen to this unpleasantness, Rose. You will regret what you've said so I would rather not hear it." And she put her hands over her ears.

Roseanne looked in increasing horror from one to the other. Rose's face was twisted with rage, her cheeks blotchy and her eyes blazing; all that could be seen of Anne was the back of her gleaming hair.

Roseanne sat in front of the mirror twisting her hands in confusion. Eventually she could keep quiet no longer. "Oh, why can't you just be friends!" she said. "And why can't I just be me!"

This was such a peculiar idea that Rose stopped screaming and Anne turned to face her. Both of them looked at Roseanne in astonishment.

Rose was the first to speak, or rather scream. "But I am you!" she shrieked, beating her fists on the glass. "You'll never get rid of me!"

"And you'll never get rid of me, either," said Anne, smiling priggishly. "I am the voice of your conscience, and I'm with you for ever."

Roseanne burst into tears. "But I don't want to be either of you!" she sobbed. Then she thought that was rather rude so she continued. "That is, I don't want to be either of you all the time," she sobbed. "There are bits of each of you that I like, but only bits."

"But you can't take bits of us!" they both said. "What would you do with the other bits?"

Roseanne felt in complete despair. "I don't know," she said, sadly. "You see I liked making the breakfast – but not every morning. And I liked being nice to old ladies, and I liked getting good marks at school – but I didn't like telling tales or washing my clothes.

"And as for you," she said to Rose, "I liked staying in bed in the morning and I liked making my friends laugh, but I didn't like breaking into the orang-utan's case at the museum and I definitely didn't like stealing from the shop."

"It was only a chocolate bar," said Rose, sulkily. "And you wouldn't have gone to prison."

"It doesn't matter," said Anne, piously. "You would have done wrong."

Roseanne started to cry again and covered her face with her hands. "Oh, I wish you'd be friends," she said. "Couldn't you at least shake hands? I'd feel so much better."

"I'll shake hands, of course, my dear, if it

would make you feel better," said Anne. "But I'm afraid Rose would never agree. She's too naughty."

"How dare you tell me what I would or wouldn't do!" said Rose. "Anyway I'd do anything to stop Roseanne making this dreadful crying racket." She reached an extremely grubby hand with dirty fingernails into the middle mirror. Reluctantly, Anne stretched out a hand and their fingers met.

Roseanne peeped up and looked at them through her fingers. "Now shake hands properly and give each other a nice big smile," she said.

Anne managed a cold smirk and Rose rustled up a cautious grin.

"That's more like it," said Roseanne, feeling happier already. "Now how about giving each other a nice big hug and being real friends!"

Rose smiled cunningly. "A hug! A nice, big hug!" But she didn't look too friendly.

Anne smiled back at Rose. "What a nice

positive response, particularly coming from such a thoroughly naughty and irresponsible girl," she replied. "Could it be that underneath, your heart is really in the right place?"

And with that she slowly moved from her side mirror into the middle mirror. Rose joined her reluctantly and then they gave each other the hugest hug you've ever seen.

They hugged and hugged until Roseanne felt quite nervous. She thought Rose was going to squeeze Anne to death. They were hugging so hard, in fact, that both Rose and Anne seemed to squash into each other and soon Roseanne could only see one pair of arms, and their hair seemed intertwined with each other's and then one of their four eyes seemed to disappear leaving only three, and their two noses became one and finally there were just two eyes left – one of Anne's and one of Rose's.

Roseanne blinked and blinked again and when she opened her eyes after the second blink she got the shock of her life. Rose and Anne had completely disappeared.

Only Roseanne herself stared back out of the mirror. She looked in one side mirror – and there was her left profile; she looked in the other side mirror – and there was her right profile. She looked behind her but there was nothing except the darkness of her room. And she looked back again, wondering.

Because although it was herself staring back at her, it was herself with a little bit of a difference. It was a livelier and happier Roseanne than she'd ever seen in her life. It was a Roseanne with a twinkle in her eye but a kindly smile, a Roseanne with clean but tousled hair which bounced about in a nice springy way. Her cheeks looked rosy but there was a smudge of ink on her neck.

And inside herself Roseanne felt quite, quite different.

Who do I feel like? she asked herself. I feel like me, she answered back.

The next morning she woke up when her mum called her for the second time. Although she felt she was back to being her old self, things had changed. She didn't have the ache in her tummy any more. And although she rather wished it were Friday so the next day would be the weekend, she didn't actually mind going to school. She pulled on her clothes and cleaned her teeth and as she looked in the mirror she suddenly thought her hair would look nicer if she pulled a bit of it up and tied a bow on it. When she found a ribbon she suddenly heard Rose's voice inside herself saying: "Hey, why not cut off all your hair and go in to school completely bald instead! What a laugh!" And then she heard Anne saying: "Oh, Roseanne, don't tie your hair up in a ribbon, your mother might not like it. Ask her first and see what she says." And although she listened to what each of them had to say and thought Rose was right to agree it should be changed and Anne was right to think it shouldn't be changed too

much, she still went ahead and tied a little bit of hair up on top of her head and then went down to breakfast.

Mum turned round from the stove. "My goodness!" she said. "What have you done with your hair?" Then she looked again. "On second thoughts, it looks quite nice. Here are your cornflakes."

Roseanne added milk and sugar – and ate them all up and had a second helping. As she put her bowl and spoon in the sink she saw her mother's eyes bulging. "You've eaten the lot!" she said. "And you had two helpings! Are you all right?"

"Fine," said Roseanne, giving her mum a great big hug and looking at her watch. "I'm late!" she said in panic. "It was that second bowl of cornflakes!"

Dad came down – and stared at her. "I like your hair, pet," he said.

"And she's eaten her cornflakes, two bowls of them," said her mum. "But now she's late for school. Still," she added, wonderingly, "at least you haven't asked if you can be let off school this morning!"

"I'll give you a lift, pet," said her dad. "I'm going that way."

At school everything went just fine. Miss Parker was a bit cross that Roseanne hadn't done more work on her project – "but," she added, "I only say that because it's so good and it's a shame to spoil it." Sharon and Wendy were most curious and impressed with her hair and wanted to copy it.

"Why don't we sneak off to the shops at break and buy some ribbon?" they said.

"Then you can show us how to put it up like that."

Inside herself Roseanne heard Anne saying: "Oh, no that wouldn't be a good idea at all, that's against the rules" but then Rose said: "Come on, you stuck up little soppy-pants, it's only five minutes!"

When they got to the shop and had bought the ribbon, Rose whispered inside her: "Hey, this is fun, let's stay here and skip school all afternoon" but Anne said: "Come on, it would only mean trouble. Let's get back." And they went back.

Over lunch Wendy and Sharon actually sat next to her and Roseanne told them about her idea of the school cooks' meetings when they all swapped recipes for disgusting food. Wendy laughed so much she spluttered over her soup. "And they probably have a special method of stitching the gristle onto the meat, they probably buy it separately and thread it through!" she said.

"And I bet they buy the skin that goes on

custard separately in sheets," said Sharon, "and spread it over the top after they've cooked it!"

Roseanne had more fun over lunch than she'd had for the last three terms at school. In the playground afterwards she played a special skipping game with Sharon, and Gemma asked her what you called a deer with only one eye* and she asked Gemma what you called the same deer with no legs.**

* no idea   ** still no idea

She was just looking at her watch realizing that for the first time in ages she'd actually stayed on for three quarters of an hour in the playground after school instead of speeding straight home as usual, when Sharon said: "Oh, just wait till my mum comes, Roseanne, I want to ask her if you can come to my party, it's silly, I mean if we can fit twenty in, we must be able to fit twenty-one." And when Sharon's mum came but protested, Sharon begged and pleaded so much she had to say yes and Sharon wrote Roseanne an invitation on the spot.

Roseanne ran all the way home because she knew she was late and when she got to the bottom of her street she saw her mum and her dad looking over the gate for her.

Mum came running down the street towards her and gave her a great big hug. "Where were you?" she asked, "We've been worried sick. I thought I'd never see my daughter again!"

"*My* daughter," said Dad, coming up and

taking her hand.

And inside Rosanne could hear Anne saying: "We must honour and obey our parents and respect them, they are our elders and betters!" and Rose saying: "Parents! Stupid soppy grown-ups, complete idiots!"

And Roseanne just looked up at her mum and her dad and gave them each a great big kiss.